D1476154

# I am NOT a Bear

for *Boo*

and all the *"Bennies"* of the world
May you always let the world know exactly who you are.

## Lisa Chong

### illustrated by Daniella Kovalerchik

Bennie had lived in the zoo her whole life.  She enjoyed having people visit her and talk to her.

But she was tired of everyone referring to her as a koala *bear*.  Bennie decided it was up to her to tell everyone the truth.

So the next day, Bennie set out to spread the word among the other animals that she is not a bear.

The orca killer whale was sleeping so Bennie tiptoed quietly, not wanting to disturb him.

Unfortunately, Bennie tripped and fell, waking the giant animal.

"Please don't hurt me," Bennie pleaded.
"Why do you think I would hurt you?" asked the orca.
"Because you're a killer whale," Bennie said. "You like to attack things."

"I'm not violent," the orca replied softly. "I don't deserve to be called a killer whale. I don't go around killing things. Besides I'm not a whale. I'm a dolphin."

"Really!" Bennie said excitedly. She thought she was the only animal others were confused about.

"I understand! I'm not a bear. I'm a marsupial!" exclaimed Bennie.

"What's a mar-soo-pal?" asked the orca.

"A marsupial," corrected Bennie. "You know, like a kangaroo. I have a pouch,"

As the two agreed to pass along their new knowledge, the shark swam up to them.

"Is the shark your cousin?" asked Bennie.

"We're not related," the shark snarled. "He's a mammal.  I'm a fish."

Bennie explained how others mistook her for a bear when she is, in fact, a marsupial.

"Like a kangaroo," the orca said, as the shark nodded understandingly.

The three agreed to help each other out and inform all the animals they met the truth about themselves and each other.

Next Bennie went to the cave where the bats live.

She stood in front of one of them and said, "I'm Bennie the koala. I am not a bear."

"But your face looks just like a bear," the bat replied.
"How do you know?" Bennie demanded. "You're blind."
"I most certainly am not," declared the bat. "I have excellent vision."

The bat told Bennie that people often believe
that bats are blind.  But bats can see.

Bennie went on to explain how a koala is not a bear,
it's a marsupial, like a kangaroo.  An orca is not a
whale, it's a dolphin and a shark is not a mammal, like
a whale or dolphin, it's a fish.

The bat promised to tell everyone she saw what she had learned, and Bennie traveled on.

Bennie next headed to the home of the ostrich, which immediately ran away and placed it's head close to the ground.

"Don't bury your head in the sand!" Bennie
called out. "I just want to tell you something."

"Ostriches don't bury their heads in the sand," said the ostrich.

"We just keep our head and neck close to the ground to hide from danger. Whoever started that rumor doesn't know ostriches!"

Wow, thought Bennie, *another animal that people make mistakes about.* She quickly relayed how a koala is not a bear, it's a marsupial. An orca is not a whale, it's a dolphin, a shark is not a mammal, it's a fish, and a bat is not blind.

The two agreed to spread the word about each other, and Bennie went on her way.

For the rest of the afternoon, Bennie visited other animals and let them know she is not a bear, but a marsupial, like a kangaroo, and showed them her pouch.

She also learned a lot of things that she had not known before.

She learned that a chameleon changes color not to camouflage itself, but to match its mood or to communicate.
A daddy longlegs is not a spider, and a penguin can come in more colors than just black and white.

As Bennie made her way home, she saw
a creature that she didn't recognize.

"Are you a fox or a raccoon?" she asked.
"I'm neither," replied the creature.
"I am a red panda."

"You're a bear?" asked Bennie.
"Just because I share the same
name as a panda bear doesn't
make me a bear like you."

"Well just because I look like a
bear doesn't make me one
either," said Bennie.

"If you're not a bear then what are you?" asked the red panda.

Bennie told her story and all her new friends' stories to the red panda like she had so many times before.

"Like a kangaroo, huh?" mused the red panda.

Bennie no longer had to worry that she'd be called a bear.

But her problems weren't over yet...

## About the author

Lisa's interest in writing stems from her enjoyment in watching emerging and reluctant readers discover the joy of books. She especially likes creating stories which allow kids who may be overlooked, the chance to discover their own special gifts. She combines her love of reading with another one of her passions, dogs, at her son's school, where she manages a reading program partnering struggling readers with dogs.

*Thanks to everyone who proofread, gave feedback and offered suggestions. Special thanks to Gabrielle for challenging me to write a story about koalas.*

## About the illustrator

Daniella is a typical middle schooler living in California's Silicon Valley. She enjoys vaulting, dancing, and of course, all aspects of art, particularly drawing. She has been drawing since the age of 5 so this is her 8th year of practicing. Daniella has a cat, but being a great vaulter and considering the horse as one of the most graceful animals, she dreams...to own her own horse. This is Daniellla's first book and she hopes to illustrate many more to come.

*Daniella says, "The joy and inspiration illustrating the book was passed on to me by my amazing teacher, Connie Zhao."*

Made in the USA
Charleston, SC
06 July 2013